4/95

dearest merry & jim,

thank you for years of
laughter and great conversation!
and for finding "Rawita".

all my love,
Laurie

Ravita and the Land of Unknown Shadows

Story by Marietta Abrams and Peter Brill
Illustrations by Laurie Smollett Kutscera

Universe Publishing

$\mathcal{L}$ong ago, nestled in the rocky cliffs of an ancient canyon, lived a people called the Anxious Ones. They were so anxious and fearful that they lived each day exactly the same.

Each morning, as the sun slid over the edge of the eastern canyon wall, they arose to their tasks. They tended the narrow ledges of cornfields that jutted out from the side of the canyon. They gathered roots and berries among the low bushes. They herded goats along the rocky slopes. And they fished in the river that coursed in a thin wedge far, far below their canyon homes.

When the sun reached the middle of the sky, the Anxious Ones retired to their homes for their mid-day supper. When the sun set atop the sheer cliff high above their homes and evening's first star appeared, they looked up into the slight stretch of sky between their canyon walls; the Anxious Ones hoped that the next day would be as uneventful as the last.

Why the Anxious Ones were so anxious

Theirs was a very peaceful existence. But when the sun set, fear spread throughout the Village. This was the time when shadows appeared, wavering and fluttering against the opposite wall of the canyon.

On some nights, the shadows barely moved. Other evenings, they swooped across the wall like wild birds. This shape they called Raggedy Bird Shadow. Sometimes, they jumped about like frantic rabbits, which they called Crazy Rabbit Shadow. There were many other shadow beings — Smiling Snake Shadow, Lunging Goat, and Shaking Juniper, to name a few.

The Anxious Ones were very scared of these dark beings. They cringed at the terrible rasping and grating sounds they made. No matter how often the villagers shouted or threatened, the Shadows kept up their devilish dance.

What made these shadows? Since they appeared on the canyon wall across from the Anxious Ones' Village, they must come from somewhere above the cliffs, above the trees, above their homes. These cliffs rose straight up from the Village. There were no paths or footholds leading up the sheer rock. No one had dared venture above their cliff dwellings to the land long called the Land of Unknown Shadows. As far back as anyone could remember, the Anxious Ones feared that the shadow beings would swoop down and destroy their Village. So each night they prayed for safety:

Oh stars so bright, so known
keep the safety of our homes!
Protect us from our fearsome foes
in the Land of Unknown Shadows!

One did not feel the same

There was one among the Anxious Peoples who did not cower from the Land of Unknown Shadows. Her name was Ravita, the youngest daughter of the oldest man in the Village. Although only a young girl, Ravita was known throughout the Village for her talents as a basket weaver. Her beautiful baskets had many uses. The small baskets were so tightly woven that they could carry water. The large baskets were so sturdy, even the most protective mother kept her infant within.

The Anxious Peoples knew that Ravita was different. She asked odd questions about the Land of Unknown Shadows. "How do we know it is bad?" she asked. "Has anyone ever explored the Land of Unknown Shadows?" Ravita had a deep desire to find the source of the wondrous shadow shapes she saw and the creaking, rasping, eerie sounds she heard.

At sunset, Ravita would sneak to the edge of the canyon and stare at the opposite wall until the shadows appeared. After a time Ravita began to know these sounds and shapes by heart, and her fear dissolved. She wasn't even afraid of Smiling Snake, the most frightening of shadows. *How silly to fear a noise or a shadow,* she thought.

One night, as she lay in the velvet silence of night, Ravita had an idea. She would climb out of the canyon, above the trees, above the cliffs and above the Village homes, and she would see for herself.

So each day Ravita escaped from her work. "I must go pick vines and reeds for my baskets," Ravita would say to her mother. But she did not go to her usual place at the river. Instead, she went to the edge of the Village, where the wall below the Land of Unknown Shadows started at the ground and rose clear up to the top. And Ravita did not use all of the reeds and roots for baskets. She decided to weave a ladder...a ladder that would stretch up the cliff that led to the Land of Unknown Shadows. Ravita carved wooden poles for the sides of the ladder. She wove the rungs using the strongest vines and reeds. It was hard weaving with these thick, thorny vines and reeds, and often her hands would bleed. But the ladder must be strong, and Ravita's will to see the Land of Unknown Shadows gave her energy. Each day, rain or shine, Ravita would go to the cliff and make one new step of the ladder.

One day, as Ravita was weaving away, she heard a sound from the brush. Quickly, Ravita covered the ladder with reeds and dirt. It was her younger cousin, Santi. "What are you doing so far from the village, Ravita? Why are you standing near the cliff?"

Ravita's voice was calm. "This is a special place where I gather vines and roots for my weaving,"she said. Ravita was happy that she did not need to lie.

"Could you teach me?" asked Santi, looking down at the ground.

"Yes, but this is my special weaving place, and you must not tell anyone about it."

Santi had never seen her cousin look so serious. "I won't tell anyone."

"Then I will show you how to make a basket of your very own." Ravita took Santi's hand and led her back to the Village.

Finally, after two moons, Ravita had all but finished her task. She was excited, but very tired. It was a wondrous ladder. Lying on the ground, it measured one hundred paces. Now came the final test. With all of her strength, Ravita lifted the ladder and propped it up against the cliff.

The ladder stood as tall as a tree. Like a deer stepping into a stream, Ravita stepped lightly onto it. She tested each rung with her full weight. She climbed and climbed, so proud of her sturdy ladder that she almost forgot her goal: the Land of Unknown Shadows. But just before reaching the top, Ravita heard a sound from below. It was Santi, singing on the path that led from the Village to the ladder. Ravita would have to either go up, or go back down. She decided to go down the ladder and meet Santi. She would wait until the next night, the night of the big Harvest Day celebration. After the festival, her family would be tired. She could easily leave her Village to explore the Land of Unknown Shadows.

A Harvest Day to remember

All through the next day, Ravita could barely concentrate on all of the Harvest Day plans. She was lost in thoughts about visiting the Land of Unknown Shadows. "What is wrong with you, Ravita?" her mother asked. "If you don't stop these foolish ways, the Unknown Shadows will snatch you away forever!" Ravita's mother had often given her such warnings when she wasn't behaving. Now Ravita just smiled to herself.

Ravita was happy that she had waited until after the Harvest Day to climb into the Land of Unknown Shadows. Harvest Day was a glorious holiday. On this day, the Village showed its thanks for the bounty of their valley, for the new children born during the year...and for their safety from the Land of Unknown Shadows. The Villagers spent weeks preparing for this celebration. They cooked rare delicacies, they cleaned their homes and they sewed fine clothes.

This Harvest Day was cool and bright. Everyone in the Village wore their most beautiful and colorful costumes. Music from bells, flutes and drums filled the air from morning to night. A ceremonial meal, served on Ravita's most beautiful baskets, was shared among the Villagers and eaten with great joy.

Just as the sun was setting, three loud drum beats sounded—*b-rum, b-rum, b-rum*—the signal for the moment that all the Villagers awaited. The Dance of the Shadow Chasers. This was the ceremony in which the Village showed its strength against the shadow beings. Every year, one child from the Village was chosen to join the Shadow Chasers, and to be an honored protector of the Village and its bounties.

$\mathcal{A}$ half circle of fire was built at the bottom of the cliff. At first pattering softly and slowly, the drums pounded louder and more quickly. *B-rum-bum...B-RUM-BUM...B-RUM-BUM...*

As the night fell, the entire Village gathered around the ring waiting for the Dance of the Shadow Chasers. Finally, the Villagers heard a rustling and rasping... then, slipping up through the bushes, the Shadow Chasers pounced into the fire ring.

First came the most fearsome Raggedy Bird Shadow Chaser, covered with dark feathers and wearing a beak woven from yellow straw. Raggedy Bird danced slowly, lunging toward the fire to make his shadow loom large against the wall.

He was soon joined by Smiling Snake Shadow Chaser, slithering and hissing along the ground, twirling high above him a long, swirling tail made of rattles green, yellow and red.

Then came Crazy Rabbit Shadow Chaser hopping in a herky-jerky way, back and forth across the wall.

A tangle of juniper branches then shook into view. It was Juniper Shadow Chaser, dotted with blue corn kernels.

Soon, all of the Shadow Chasers were together in the fire ring, dancing to the pounding drum. Their dances cast shadows that were wild, fearful and beautiful all at the same time.

The drums pounded more slowly as the Shadow Chasers spread out along the edge of the fire ring. The children of the Village stood in the front row, closest to the fire and the Shadow Chasers. They waited breathlessly to see which of them would be chosen to join the Shadow Chasers. Ravita felt the warmth of the fire on her face, and her hands tingled with excitement.

Suddenly, with a whoop and a rustle of feathers, Raggedy Bird Shadow Chaser spread his wings. The other Shadow Chasers stepped back. Raggedy Bird whirled around and cried a screeching call, *A-rri!!*. His wings turned slowly, slowly across the children's faces. Which one would it be? Which child would become a Shadow Chaser? Raggedy Bird's wings fluttered high into the sky and, with another piercing screech, swooped down around Ravita! Ravita felt the soft feathers graze her shoulders. She smelled the straw of Raggedy Bird's beak. In that dark and exciting moment, Ravita knew what to do. Trembling, Ravita stepped into the center of the fire ring.

Ravita's heart was beating as quickly as a hummingbird's wings. All of the Shadow Chasers danced around her, each giving her a piece of their costume: Juniper Tree Shadow Chaser draped branches around Ravita's neck. Smiling Snake placed rattles in her hands. Crazy Rabbit ringed her ankles in milkweed. Finally, Raggedy Bird Shadow Chaser placed a wreath of feathers around her head. "You are now a Shadow Chaser and honored protector of the Anxious Ones' Village." The Villagers clapped and cheered.

Ravita raised her arms into the air and began the dance that would best show her feelings about being a Shadow Chaser. She first swooped down, then fluttered her arms like a bird. She turned her head left then right, spread her arms aloft and glided quickly around and around the fire ring. In keeping with the tradition, Ravita announced her name. "I am Soaring Dove Shadow Chaser," Ravita cried. "And I will protect my Village with peace and grace."

Ravita's willowy shadow played lightly against the canyon wall.

After the festivities, the villagers gathered around the central fire for the final evening prayer. Ravita's father, the oldest member and leader of the Anxious Ones, led the song:

Thank you Stars for your evening light.
Thank you Sun for your beauty bright.
Thank you Earth for the food you give.
Thank you, thank you for the life we live.

*A*ll of the Anxious Ones returned to their homes. They were tired and happy after a successful Harvest Festival. The entire Village soon was asleep. Only Ravita was wide awake. Becoming a Shadow Chaser had only given her more reason to visit the Land of Unknown Shadows. "I will see for myself, and as Ravita the Soaring Dove Shadow Chaser, I will make peace with the Land of Unknown Shadows."

Ravita slipped from her bed quietly, took her Shadow Chaser costume and ran to her woven ladder at the cliff wall. She climbed, certain this time that her ladder would not break. Halfway up the ladder, Ravita looked down. The night was lit by the moon and stars. Ravita could see her Village nestled into the canyon wall. In the far distance she could even see the warm glow of the fire ring. For the first time, Ravita was frightened, but she kept climbing.

Ravita had nearly reached the top. Her heart was drumming in her chest. She looked up. Above the canyon walls, the sky seemed hugely vast and filled with more stars than she had ever seen before. The more she looked, the more she noticed the stars flying through the sky in a crazy kind of way. Being so close to such grandness made Ravita feel very small and alone. A chill tickled up and down her back as Ravita stepped into the Land of Unknown Shadows.

Where is Ravita?

"Where is Ravita?" were the first words out of her mother's mouth the morning after Harvest Day.

"Oh, that lazy squirrel," said Ravita's father. "She is probably still sleeping. After all, becoming a Shadow Chaser does not happen every day. Let the girl have her rest."

At noontime, when Ravita had still not appeared, her parents became worried and looked into her room. Their daughter was nowhere to be found. Ravita's parents decided to call a Village meeting.

"Ravita is missing," said the girl's mother. "She has not been seen since the Harvest Day celebration! We must find her." A hush came over the Village. They were all thinking the same thing: *Ravita, the Village's youngest Shadow Chaser, had been snatched up into the Land of Unknown Shadows.*

The Anxious Ones looked throughout the nooks and crannies of the cliff dwellings. They searched dark caves, they forged through streams. "Ravita! Ravita! Ravita!" echoed throughout the canyon.

Suddenly, cousin Santi remembered, "I think I know where she might be." Ravita's mother kneeled down and took Santi's hand. "Little one, what do you know about this?" Santi then told everyone about the day she had found Ravita at the cliff, picking vines and roots.

"Show us!" said Ravita's mother. And Santi led everyone along the path to Ravita's special place.

It was getting late. The shadows were beginning to creep down the canyon wall. There was a woven ladder lying flat on the ground. Ravita's mother looked closely at it. "Only Ravita could have woven this," she said. "But where is Ravita?" The Anxious Ones looked, following the cliff's sheer wall up, up, up to the Land of Unknown Shadows. Together, they lifted the ladder and leaned it against the wall. Sure enough, it reached just to the top of the cliff.

The Anxious Ones stood in silence at the bottom of the ladder. The sun would soon set over the edge of the canyon. A hollow *whoop* sounded from the dark, high horizon. Across the canyon, a new shape fluttered against the wall; it was a willowy shadow that looked somehow familiar.

"I must go now to the Land of Unknown Shadows and find my daughter," said Ravita's father.

But Ravita's mother objected. "No, the Village needs its leader. You stay with them. I will find Ravita."

She climbed, one rung after the next, up the sturdy woven ladder. Even in her fear and worry, Ravita's mother could not help admiring her daughter's fine work. Every few steps she turned back to look at the graceful shadow playing against the canyon wall.

Then Ravita's mother stepped onto the Land of Unknown Shadows. For the first time in her life, there was no canyon wall stopping her view.

Ravita's mother saw juniper and pine trees. She smelled sage and thyme. *The Land of Unknown Shadows is just like home, except more spread out,* she thought.

Then Ravita's mother looked up and out to the new, flat horizon. The sun was burning purple and orange. Soon it would be dark.

Ravita's mother searched the landscape for her daughter. She walked slowly through brush and bramble, calling "Ravita! Ravita!" The sounds of branches scraping in the wind were her only answer. A family of deer was drinking from a small stream. The animals looked up in surprise and galloped into the distance.

Then Ravita's mother turned toward the canyon edge. An unusual shape, neither tree nor bush, flailed wildly in the wind. But in all its strangeness, this form reminded her of something. It's head was swathed in feathers, its body covered with juniper branches and its ankles ringed with milk-weed. It was Ravita dressed in her Shadow Chaser costume! She was dancing her Soaring Dove Shadow Dance, moving her arms to and fro. "Ravita!" she called, and ran to the edge of the canyon.

"Mother! I'm so happy to see you," Ravita cried. "My ladder fell but I knew you would find me!" Ravita's mother ran to her daughter and hugged her tightly. Ravita pointed to the canyon wall opposite the Land of the Unknown Shadows. "Look! It's the most amazing thing!" Ravita raised her arm and the graceful shadow on the opposite wall did the same. She took her mother's hand and two shapes were joined on the canyon wall. Then Ravita and her mother danced for joy.

From down below, all the Anxious Ones in the Village saw two birds dancing on the canyon wall.

First published in the United States of America in 1994
by UNIVERSE PUBLISHING
300 Park Avenue South
New York, NY 10010
Story and text © 1994 by Marietta Abrams and Peter Brill
Illustrations © 1994 by Laurie Smollett Kutscera

Book design by Jennifer Eisenpresser
94 95 96 97 98 99/ 10 9 8 7 6 5 4 3 2 1
Printed in Hong Kong

Library of Congress Cataloging-In-Publication data
Abrams, Marietta.
Ravita and the Land of Unknown Shadows/Marietta Abrams and Peter Brill
illustrations by Laurie Smollett Kutscera.
p.   cm.
Summary: The Anxious Ones, whose village is deep within a canyon, are all frightened of
the shadows from the unknown land on the cliffs above, except for Ravita, who longs to
climb up above the cliffs to see for herself what is there.
ISBN: 0-87663-793-4
[1. Fear—Fiction. 2. Courage—Fiction. 3. Shadows—Fiction.]
I. Brill, Peter. II. Kutscera, Laurie Smollett, ill. III. Title.
PZ7.B7662Rav 1994
[Fic]—dc20   94-6901 CIP AC